A NOSE FOR TRUFFLES

CLAIRE OWERS

Thank you as ever to Christy Johnson for her wonderful cover art.

www.christy-johnson.com

A special mention also goes to the Wallace family for naming the pig - Soufflé is a brilliant choice! Thank you.

For more fun, competitions and news you can sign up to my mailing list at
www.claireowersauthor.com
I'll even send you a free activity sheet!

For everyone at Drumoak Primary School...

Books by Claire Owers:

Monty: A Nose for Trouble
Monty: A Nose for Treasure
Monty: A Nose for Truffles

CONTENTS

1

Calais

Megan slid the window open, and a rush of warm, unfamiliar air filled the van. Monty's nose twitched at the sudden fresh smells. He barged his snout past Megan to take it all in, his chest straining against his little doggy seatbelt. Megan was sure he would love to be leaning out of the window with his tongue hanging out, like the dogs you see in movies. But Dad said that was dangerous. Peering past Monty's fluffy ears, Megan watched the procession of vehicles snake towards the main road, an assortment of number plates on display; GB: Great Britain, F: France, I: Italy, and some that she couldn't figure out. *Where was D from?* she wondered as a sleek Mercedes sped past them. She was just about to ask Mum when Nicole snatched the tattered French phrasebook from her knee.

'I was using that!' Megan protested.

'No, you weren't! You were looking out of the window!' Nicole retorted.

'What are you looking up, anyway?' asked Megan, sliding the window shut.

'*Sortie*...' Nicole muttered.

'It means 'exit' Nicole, has Mrs Thomas not taught you that?'

'*Yes*. I just forgot, Megan,' Nicole huffed.

'Girls, please stop bickering,' Mum sighed from the front seat.

'It's been a *long* journey,' Dad grumbled. 'Driving on the wrong side of the road is not as easy as you'd think. Our van isn't the right way round, remember. So please let me concentrate.'

'That was pretty cool driving onto the train, wasn't it?' Mum said, trying to lift the mood.

'Yes!' Megan grinned. 'I can't wait to tell everyone that I've been through the channel tunnel!'

As they hit the main road, the unpronounceable road signs began to whizz past.

'This is the van's first proper adventure!' Nicole announced.

The Bruce family were driving to a small campsite in Burgundy for the October holidays. Their transporter van, with its fold-out bed and pop-up roof, was going to be their home for the next two weeks. It was so jam-packed that Megan was surprised the sides weren't bulging. They had driven down to Kent from Aberdeen the day before and had woken up early to cross to Calais.

'How long do we have to go, Dad?' Megan asked tentatively.

'Six, maybe seven hours,' Dad replied, keeping his eyes fixed on the road.

Megan's face fell. That seemed like forever.

'We'll have plenty of stops, though,' Mum added. 'Monty will need to stretch his legs.'

'It'll be an adventure, seeing all the places along the way,' Dad said, ignoring the impatient tooting of the car behind as he tried to negotiate the chaotic traffic.

Nicole looked up from the phrasebook and clasped her hand to her nose.

'Oh Monty, not again!' groaned Mum from the front.

'It stinks!' Nicole shrieked from under her tightly clasped hand.

'I think it's just the stress of the journey…' said Mum, grimacing.

Dad pressed the button to lower his window.

'I don't think that scotch egg he picked up off the floor in the last service station helped either,' said Dad, raising his eyebrow.

'Or the cheese he stole from my sandwich,' Megan added, pinching her nose.

'Your voice sounds funny, Megan!' Nicole giggled.

'I knew we should have left him with Granny and Grandad,' Dad muttered to Mum.

'It wouldn't be a holiday without Monty!' protested Mum.

'Well, as long as he's on his best behaviour,' said Dad, giving Monty a stern glance.

Monty sat panting in the middle seat, seemingly oblivious to the stench.

2

Paris

The journey seemed to stretch on forever. Every service station was beginning to feel pretty much the same. The motorway landscape blended into one long blur of trucks and concrete, fields and sky, hotels and service stations. Before long, they had exhausted their supply of travel games and couldn't agree on which audiobook to listen to, so Dad put the radio off completely. The van fell silent. The muted hum of the traffic and the rumbling tyres on the road made Megan's eyelids feel heavy.

Something wet slid over Megan's face. It felt warm.

'Yuck! Monty!' she grumbled, on discovering that the wet thing was his tongue.

She rubbed the drool off her face with her jumper sleeve. Monty sat panting excitedly at her, clearly pleased that she was now awake. Megan wondered how long she had been asleep. The scenery outside had changed. The van was now stationary, and they appeared to be in a city. Nicole sat snoozing beside her, with her mouth hanging gently open.

'Where are we?' Megan asked. 'Are we there yet?'

'Oh hello, sleepy head,' Dad smiled. 'Not quite.'

'But look outside...can you guess where we are?' Mum grinned.

Megan looked out at the congested street.

'Look behind those buildings...in the background...'

'The Eiffel Tower! We're in Paris!' Megan gasped. 'Nicole, wake up!' she said, shoving her little sister.

'Megan!' Nicole complained.

'Look where we are, Nicole! Paris!'

'Wow!' Nicole said excitedly, rubbing the sleep from her eyes. 'Is that the Eiffel Tower?!'

Megan nodded animatedly.

'There was an accident on the road that we were planning to take, so we had to come this way instead,' explained Mum.

'Right through the centre of Paris,' said Dad, laughing nervously. 'This could be interesting!'

'It's so busy,' said Megan, looking out at the packed lanes of traffic.

'Yes. I don't think we'll be stopping, I'm afraid. We want to get through the traffic before rush hour hits,' Mum said, anxiously checking her watch.

Megan stared in awe at the circus outside her window. It was so busy! A group of children zoomed past on scooters, schoolbags on their backs, weaving their way through the crowds. Mopeds buzzed everywhere. An old lady walked past with a tiny dog in a jacket. There were cafés with fancy names printed onto canopies that stretched out over the street. Two men sat with tiny cups of coffee, watching the people parade past them. There were trees and dogs and posh looking boutiques and newsagents with fruit and veg colourfully displayed outside. And everyone seemed to be in such a rush!

'I wish we could go to Disneyland!' sighed Nicole dreamily, breaking Megan from her thoughts.

'That would be cool,' agreed Megan. 'Milly went there last summer, and she said the Pirates of the Caribbean ride was amazing!'

'Maybe next year…' said Mum.

'But hey, camping is *so* much more fun than Disneyland!' Dad announced, his enthusiasm almost infectious.

Suddenly a moped sped past Megan's window, its engine whining loudly. They watched as the moped mounted the pavement to nip past the queuing traffic.

'Is that allowed?' Nicole gasped.

'I'm not sure,' said Mum, 'but it's very dangerous!'

'Hopefully, not much further until we get back onto the motorway!' said Dad.

3

Burgundy

Four hours later, they finally pulled up at the campsite. It should have been three hours, but the sat nav had got confused when they reached the narrow streets of the town. Eventually, they had stopped and asked a kind French lady, who had pointed them in the right direction.

They were allocated a peaceful pitch under a hazel tree. The air was cool now, with the sun low in the sky, but the birds and insects hummed happily all around them. The campsite was full of the noise of families preparing their evening meals. Smoky barbecue smells filled the air.

Dad had given them each a task to do so that they could get set up quickly. Megan took a big breath in and sighed out happily as she set up all the camping chairs.

'I'm so glad we're finally here!' she smiled, plonking herself down in a chair.

'Me too!' said Mum, wrestling with the awning. 'And I think we made pretty good time, especially with that diversion!'

'It was quite a pleasant drive after that madness!' Dad shouted down from inside the van.

He shoved the roof open. It looked like a crocodile's mouth, ready to go snap.

'Right, your bedroom is ready girls!'

'Thanks, Dad,' smiled Nicole, as she got to work setting up Monty's doggy tent.

Monty sniffed excitedly around her, getting himself completely in the way.

'Monty, you're making this much harder!' Nicole scolded playfully.

'Let me help with that,' said Mum, as one of the poles sprang up and whacked Nicole on the head.

'Yes, please!' she laughed.

Before long, the van was all set, and Monty's tent was finally up. He leapt in and out of it in excitement.

'Right!' said Dad, clapping his hands. 'Time for food!'

4

Un Cochon

Megan slurped her Fanta down happily as they sat waiting for their food to arrive. They had decided to go out for dinner tonight as a treat after the journey. The campsite had three restaurants, a shop and a bakery. There were even tennis courts and a swimming pool!

'Isn't this lovely?' smiled Mum, leaning back in her chair.

'Yes, it's a brilliant campsite. Well chosen!' said Dad, clinking Mum's glass with his own.

'What do you girls fancy doing tomorrow?' asked Mum. 'We could try and find the cycle path and explore the...' Mum's voice trailed off. 'What on earth?'

'Well, I've seen it all now...' muttered Dad in disbelief, staring at something behind the girls.

Both sisters whipped round to see what their parents were staring at.

'Is that... a pig?!' Nicole gasped.

'A pig on a lead!' tittered Megan.

The girls fell into fits of giggles.

'Girls, don't laugh!' Mum hissed, although she was struggling to keep her own face straight.

A large gentleman walked casually past the restaurant complex with a wicker basket in one hand and a lead in the other. On the end of the lead was a pig. A huge, hairy, pink pig.

'Why is he taking a pig for a walk?' said Nicole, still full of giggles.

All of a sudden, the table jolted abruptly, causing their drinks to slop over the sides of their glasses.

'Monty! NO!' Dad said firmly.

But it was too late. Monty's lead slipped off the table leg where it had been anchored. With his eyes fixed on the strangest dog he had ever seen, Monty bolted from the seating area. The girls cringed as Monty charged towards the man and his pig. The couple at the table next to them gawked at the spectacle. Mum and Dad were already sprinting after Monty.

'This could end badly,' said Megan, biting hard on her fingernail.

'Come on. We need to catch up!' ordered Nicole, dragging Megan out of her seat.

Monty bounced excitedly up to the pig, with his tail wagging hopefully. As he came snout to snout with the animal, it let out a tremendous shriek. Monty jumped back, and his tail went between his legs. The pig stamped its trotters on the earth, grunting angrily. It did not seem pleased.

The man seemed even less pleased. He was shouting something in French, but Megan couldn't understand. She had never heard some of the words he was using.

'Je suis désolé...' said Mum in her best French, raising her hands in apology. 'My dog... err...*mon chien,* est très excitè...He's never seen a... *cochon* before,' she stammered, gesturing at the pig.

The man looked confused.

'I think Monty thought the *cochon* was a dog,' added Nicole, looking up at the man. 'Un cochon, un chien,' Nicole shrugged, tilting her head from side to side.

Megan tried not to laugh at her sister's French accent.

The man looked down at her with his brow furrowed. He had deep lines on his face and leathery skin that looked like it had spent a lifetime under the hot sun. Although he was cross, he had kind eyes.

'Soufflé is very obviously, a *pig*. She is a very special pig. Much more intelligent than your dog,' he harrumphed.

'We really are sorry, monsieur,' said Dad.

Monty had gone into hiding behind Mum's legs. Every now and then he would peek round to eye the strange, shrieking dog. It stared back at him with its little piggy eyes, making grunting noises. It seemed to have calmed down.

'Why is Soufflé special?' asked Megan.

'Ah, Soufflé is a hunter,' the man said with a twinkle in his eye.

'What does she hunt?' Nicole asked with a gulp. She hoped it wasn't Labradors.

'The treasure of Burgundy,' the man said with a wink.

He was being very mysterious. But Megan had been reading about the treasure of Burgundy in her guidebook on the way here.

'Soufflé is a truffle hog, isn't she?' she grinned.

'Ah-ha! You've got it child, bravo!'

'A truffle hog?' asked Nicole, screwing her face up. 'Pigs like chocolate?'

'Madame! Monsieur! Your food is here!' called the waiter from the restaurant.

'Oh! We'd better go and eat,' said Mum. 'Come on, girls. Say bye to the gentleman and, erm, Soufflé.'

The girls smiled goodbye. Soufflé gave a parting grunt as Monty scurried back towards the restaurant and the safety of underneath the table.

5

Breakfast

The following morning, Megan watched as the sausages sizzled and popped. Dad grabbed two with the tongs and deposited them onto her plate.

'Thanks, Dad,' she smiled.

Mum was rummaging about in the back of the van.

'That's the last of Monty's kibble gone,' she called, holding up the empty food box.

'Ah yes. I forgot to say, I used the last of it for his tea last night.' said Dad apologetically.

'Right girls, finish your breakfast, then you can head to the campsite shop. I'm sure they'll have some small bags.'

'Ok,' Megan mumbled, through a mouthful of food.

'Best not feed him any sausages after what his tummy has been like,' Mum said, raising an eyebrow as Dad was about to drop a piece of sausage under the table.

Monty let out a long sigh.

The girls skipped happily through the rows of tents and caravans. Nicole had the campsite map, and Megan had hold of Monty's lead.

'Look at that house,' said Nicole, intrigued. 'It's not on the map.'

Behind the pitches, a little cottage was nestled in a clump of trees.

'It must not belong to the campsite,' shrugged Megan.

They stopped and peered over the wall into the overgrown garden. Plants weaved their way up the side of the building and twisted around the window shutters.

'Oh, it's that grumpy old man again,' said Nicole. 'The one that had the pig… Suzy, or whatever it was called, that likes chocolate.'

'Soufflé,' corrected Megan. 'And Burgundy truffles are not the same as chocolate truffles, they're like a kind of mushroom that grows underground.'

Nicole rolled her eyes at her big sister.

'Know-all! Sounds yuck anyway.'

'Anyway,' Megan continued, ignoring her little sister. 'I think he's a nice man…maybe just not a dog person.'

'You only like him because he was impressed with your pig knowledge,' teased Nicole.

'You were the one speaking French to him, remember!' Megan laughed.

'Sssh, he's coming over,' hissed Nicole.

'Why are you two prying into my property?' he said, frowning. 'I hope you don't have that dog with you again. He must not come near my Soufflé!'

Megan gulped.

'See, told you he was grumpy,' whispered Nicole.

'Sorry monsieur,' stuttered Megan, hoping that the man couldn't see Monty tucked behind the garden wall. 'We were just having a look around the campsite...Is this your house? Your garden is lovely...' She smiled weakly, tightening her grip on Monty's lead.

'What's that smell?' asked Nicole, screwing her nose up.

The sudden questioning seemed to distract the man from his scolding of them.

'Ah. I am making cheese... *fromage de chévre*. It is a speciality!'

The smell was drifting out of an open door. Megan felt the lead tense in her hand. *Oh no* she thought.

'Monty hasn't had breakfast,' she hissed to Nicole out of the side of her mouth.

Nicole gave her a confused look. Megan leaned in to say it again, but the lead tightened sharply in her hand.

'He's not had breakfast!' she yelled as Monty pulled her forwards.

'Oh! Monty, leave!' Nicole shouted, but it was in vain.

The man started ranting in French, flapping his arms around. The only words that Megan could pick out were *arrêt* and *chien*. He stomped towards Monty, with his legs and arms wide, as if he was going to rugby tackle him. But Monty zipped around the man and dragged Megan straight into the house.

6

Fromage

Megan charged into a tiny, cluttered kitchen. Beside the sink was a huge bowl with a muslin cloth inside it. The cloth contained a lumpy white mixture that smelled as unpleasant as it looked. Monty put his paws up on the worktop.

'MONTY, leave!' Megan commanded firmly.

Mustering as much energy as she could, Megan tugged sharply on his lead. Monty's paws returned to the floor, and he glanced up guiltily. Megan sighed heavily, relieved that he had come to his senses.

'Good boy. I thought we'd trained that out of you, mister!'

Monty had a history of food stealing that had landed him in trouble on several occasions. At one time, he was even banned from the school after a particularly shameful incident. The family had worked hard on his training, and now he mostly used his astonishing sense of smell as a force for good. He had even solved crimes with his nasal abilities! Cheese, however, still proved hard for him to resist. Monty gazed up at Megan with sorry amber eyes. It was hard to stay cross at him for long.

Megan looked around the crowded space. Kitchen utensils hung on the walls, and there were jars of preserved food stacked on shelves. Every surface seemed to be covered. The window wasn't letting much light in as the plants had grown over the outside of it. There was a door on the other side of the room that Megan presumed must lead to the rest of the house. On an island in the centre of the kitchen sat a wicker basket full of lumpy brown things. *Truffles!* Megan thought. They were letting off a musty aroma, but it was hard to smell anything but the stinky cheese.

Suddenly the man crashed in, closely followed by Nicole.

'Get that dog away from my truffles!' he shouted crossly.

'He's not interested in the truffles. It's the cheese, monsieur,' Megan explained, pointing to the lumpy white goop. 'I'm guessing that's cheese?' she said curiously. 'He didn't touch it though!' she added hurriedly.

'A dog who likes *cheese*?'

The man looked perplexed. He threw his head back and laughed heartily. Megan smiled awkwardly. From behind the man, Nicole gestured for her to get out.

'Anyway, I'm so sorry we barged into your house,' she went to get past the man, who was still standing in the doorway.

Suddenly there was a loud thump against the door at the back of the kitchen. Then another thump, followed by a scraping sound.

Nicole's eyes widened.

'What's that?!' she cried.

7

Soufflé

The scraping and scuffing behind the door was getting louder. Monty's hackles had gone up, and he stood on guard at Megan's side.

'What's behind that door?' asked Megan, trying to sound brave.

'Oh! That's just Soufflé!' chuckled the man.

'You keep her in the house?!' gasped Nicole.

'Why yes, of course. She is my pet. Just

like *that* is your pet,' he said, casting a disapproving look at Monty.

'Doesn't she make a mess?' Megan asked.

'She is very well trained,' said the man. 'But yes, she can get a little destructive if she is bored.'

Suddenly the door burst open. The back of the wooden door was covered in scars. The pig stood in the doorway. She filled most of the frame.

'You see,' said the man, gesturing to the battered door. 'She scrapes at things a lot.'

Soufflé let out a long grunt as she trotted towards the kitchen island and started scraping at it with her snout and trotters.

'She wants to eat the truffles. She has a rather healthy appetite and a keen sense of smell. That's why I have to keep her out of the kitchen.'

'Monty and Soufflé have quite a lot in common,' said Megan, observing the pig with fascination.

Monty tugged at his lead. He had seen enough and was desperate to skulk away. His body was as close to the floor as his legs would allow as he tried to stay hidden from the pig. But something in the dusty, old kitchen seemed to tickle his nose, and he let out a massive sneeze.

Soufflé looked up and trotted at pace straight towards Monty, ears bobbing and trotters clacking on the tiled floor. Monty cowered and closed his eyes as he once again came snout to snout with the strangest dog ever. Soufflé stood and nudged at Monty's face. He slowly opened his eyes and sniffed cautiously at her face. Soufflé let out a high pitched squeal and then licked Monty's nose.

Monty recoiled in surprise, his nose wrinkling up before he sneezed violently once again. He cocked his head to one side.

'Oh my goodness,' muttered the man in disbelief. 'She likes him. For a pig, a lick is the greatest sign of affection!'

'Oh! That's great,' said Megan, uncertainly. She looked down at Monty, who still looked very confused.

'Your dog is not a threat to my Soufflé after all. My apologies,' said the man, sounding genuinely remorseful.

'That's ok,' said Nicole, who was still standing in the hallway.

'I have had bad experiences with dogs in the past. They are predators, you see. Whereas the pig is prey.'

'I thought you said Soufflé was a hunter?' asked Nicole.

'Yes, but only of truffles! She is vulnerable to attack from other animals. Especially at the moment...' he knelt down to pat his pig, who was still nudging at Monty playfully. Monty looked quite bewildered.

'What do you mean?' asked Megan.

'She is expecting piglets!' he announced proudly.

'Aww!' said the girls in unison.

'They'll be so cute,' smiled Megan, giving Soufflé a tentative pat on the head. She had never touched a pig before.

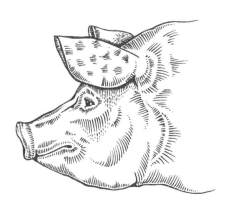

'I'm sorry. I am a bit protective of her at the moment. I haven't been very kind to you children. My wife would be very displeased.'

'Is she not home?' asked Nicole.

'Ah. No, she passed away last year…The house is very quiet without her.'

'Oh. I'm sorry,' said Nicole quietly.

Megan felt sorry for the man. She was right all along, he was kind at heart, just worried for his pet. She thought of all the times that she had fought for Monty. The love for a pet was fierce.

'We better go,' said Megan, 'Mum and Dad will be wondering where we are.'

'Of course!' said the man, ushering them out of the house.

'What's your name?' asked Nicole before they departed.

'Monsieur Hubert,' he smiled. 'I hope I haven't scared you. Please feel free to visit any time. Soufflé doesn't have many friends, and she seems to like your Monty... Your strange dog that likes cheese and is friends with a pig!' he laughed heartily to himself again.

'Monty is *un chien spécial*, Monsieur Hubert!' Megan said, hoping she'd got her pronunciation correct.

8

The Apology

'I'm not very happy about you talking to strangers, girls,' said Mum, frowning.

'He wasn't a stranger. We met him at the restaurant, remember?' said Nicole.

'I also can't believe you barged in to the man's house!' said Dad in disbelief.

'It was Monty,' Megan muttered, scuffing at something on the grass with her shoe. 'He was hungry…and the cheese was so pongy…I just couldn't stop him.'

Dad sighed loudly.

'We'll have to go round and apologise,' said Mum. 'He didn't seem like the sort of man that would take kindly to that sort of behaviour.'

Dad nodded in agreement.

'But he was ok, he wasn't upset!' protested Megan.

'Yeah, he actually thought it was funny in the end. He's not a horrible grump after all,' added Nicole.

'Yes, Monsieur Hubert is a kind man. He even came around to Monty. He was just worried that Monty was a threat to Soufflé, but…'

'That's enough,' said Dad, raising his hand. 'We'll go round and sort this out tomorrow morning.'

The next morning, the girls dragged their heels behind Mum and Dad.

'I'd rather be in the swimming pool,' Megan said quietly, looking glumly at her sister.

'Me too,' sighed Nicole.

It was a lovely sunny day and much warmer than they had been expecting for the time of year. The pool looked so inviting.

'You'll have plenty of time for that later,' said Dad. 'Now, is this the house?'

Nicole nodded.

They made their way up the overgrown path to the wooden door that Megan had clattered through the day before.

Mum knocked tentatively.

A commotion could be heard on the other side of the door. Megan smiled to herself as she pictured Monsieur Hubert shooing

Soufflé away from the door, just like they do with Monty when their doorbell goes.

'Bonjour,' Monsieur Hubert said in a questioning tone as he cast his eyes over the family on his doorstep.

'Ah, hello, Monsieur Hubert. We just wanted to apologise for our dog...well our children too, actually...entering your property yesterday. It was *very* rude. Megan, Nicole, what do you have to say to Monsieur Hubert?'

Mum had given up attempting to speak French. She sounded flustered enough trying to get the words out in English.

'Sorry Monsieur Hubert,' Megan and Nicole chimed.

'No harm done, I hope?' asked Dad cautiously.

'*Non non non!*' said Monsieur Hubert cheerfully, shaking his head. 'The girls gave me an apology yesterday. Everything is good. *Pas de problème!* You know…your girls remind me of my own grandchildren,' he said with a faraway look on his face. 'I also rather like your strange cheese-eating dog,' he chuckled to himself again.

Mum and Dad exchanged a bemused look.

'Please, come in! Soufflé would love to play with Monty. She is not herself today. She did not find a single truffle this morning! I think the pregnancy is unsettling her.'

Before Mum could politely refuse, Monsieur Hubert was ushering her inside. The girls followed on, with Dad dragging a somewhat reluctant Monty at the back.

9

Oh Là Là

Monsieur Hubert led them through to a small sitting room. It was much brighter than the kitchen, with the sunlight streaming in through the french doors. He gestured for them to take a seat. As Dad plonked himself down in an old armchair, a plume of dust puffed into the air. The dust motes danced around in the sunbeams. Megan, Nicole and Mum perched on the faded sofa. Monty sat awkwardly against Dad's legs, his tail twitching nervously.

'Café? Thé?' asked Monsieur Hubert. 'I don't have your English 'tea' I'm afraid... Or...ah, I have lovely fresh lemonade? It is very good!' he said with a smile.

'Oh, that sounds lovely!' said Mum, still looking a little unsure about the situation.

The family nodded in agreement, and Monsieur Hubert bustled off towards the kitchen.

'Well...this is rather strange,' said Dad in a hushed voice. 'It certainly wasn't on the camping itinerary!'

'He does seem like a kind man though, girls. I think you're right,' Mum said thoughtfully. 'Did he say Soufflé is pregnant?'

'Yes, she's going to have piglets!' gushed Nicole. 'How cool is that?!'

'That's lovely,' smiled Mum.

'I think Monsieur Hubert is lonely,' Megan whispered, looking at the photographs on the walls.

On the side table next to Dad, there was a beautiful, ornate gold photo frame. Megan guessed the smiling lady in the photograph was Mrs Hubert.

'Yeah, his wife died. It's just him and Soufflé,' said Nicole sadly.

'Oh, that is a shame,' said Mum.

Suddenly there was a bang against the living room door, followed by frantic scuffling and scratching.

'Soufflé!' Megan said, grinning at Nicole.

'That's the pig making that noise?' said Dad in alarm.

'Yes, but don't worry, she won't hurt you!' said Nicole.

The door slammed open, and in charged Soufflé, ears bobbing in excitement. She let out a squeal of delight as her piggy eyes found Monty. Monty jumped up onto Dad's knee in alarm.

'Oooft, Monty! Get off!' said Dad. 'You're far too big to sit on my knee.'

Monty scrabbled back onto the floor. He squeezed his eyes tight shut as Soufflé reached him. She nudged his chest playfully.

Monty opened his eyes and stared at the strange squealing dog. He wondered what it smelled like...Tentatively he reached his snout forward and took a timid sniff of Soufflé's face. Soufflé stood grunting happily.

'I think Monty's trying to figure out what she is,' laughed Mum. 'Surely he doesn't still think she's a dog?'

Dad laughed in agreement.

'I just hope he doesn't try to sniff her b…'

But before Dad could finish his sentence, chaos erupted. Monty had indeed gone one sniff too far, and Soufflé charged off around the room. The thrill of having something to chase seemed to rid Monty of his anxieties, and he took off in pursuit.

Monsieur Hubert arrived back with the lemonade. He whipped the tray upwards and out of the way just in time as Monty and Soufflé stormed past. The lemonade jug started to rock, and Monsieur Hubert had to weave around with the tray above his head to steady it.

'Oh là là! What a commotion!' he shouted above the squealing and clattering trotters and paws.

'Monty! Calm down!' scolded Dad.

At the mention of his name, Monty stopped and pricked up his ears. Soufflé blindsided him, sending him crashing into the side table next to Dad. The table swayed, and the gold photo frame on top began to wobble.

Megan dived through the air and caught the photograph just before it hit the wooden floor.

'Wow, Megan! Impressive dive!' said Nicole in awe.

'Oh, thank you! Thank you so much, young lady. That photo is very precious to me,' Monsieur Hubert said.

'It's ok,' shrugged Megan, placing the photo carefully back in place.

Her knee did sting a bit from her landing, but she was glad the photo wasn't damaged.

Monty sat sheepishly at Mum's feet as Soufflé was escorted out of the room.

'Now, lemonade!' said Monsieur Hubert on his return.

He began pouring the lemonade into glasses.

Megan took a big gulp, and immediately her face contorted into a bitter wince. It was the most sour thing she had ever tasted.

She tried to open her eyes to look at Nicole. Her sister had done the same thing. They laughed at each other's twisted up faces.

'Ah, yes, there is sugar here,' Monsieur Hubert said, pointing out a little sugar bowl and five long spoons. 'You add it to taste! It is *very* sour without sugar!' he laughed.

10

Calm Restored

'Did you say that you have grandchildren, Monsieur Hubert?' Mum asked as they sat with their, now sweetened, lemonade.

'*Oui*. A girl and a boy. Sophia and Olivier. They must be about the same age as Megan and Nicole here. They live in Paris...such a long way for me.'

'Do you not get to see them often?' Mum asked sympathetically.

'No, for me, it is too expensive to travel,' he sighed. 'They sometimes come and visit in the school holidays, but life is busy for them. You know how it is,' he smiled sadly.

'We drove through Paris!' exclaimed Nicole.

'I can't imagine what it would be like to live there,' said Megan, wide-eyed.

'It is not so different,' Monsieur Hubert shrugged. 'They live in a nice house, with a garden, not far from the city. They go to school, as you do. And they have tennis lessons in the evenings and football at the weekends. In the winter holidays, they like to go skiing. In the summer, they go camping. But they don't have a dog, they have a house cat.'

Megan thought back to the busy streets of Paris. The children going to school on their scooters, the busy traffic and the mopeds on the pavement. Despite all that, the way Monsieur Hubert explained it made it sound quite similar to their own life. Except for the cat.

Megan stroked Monty's soft head and ran his silky ear through her fingers. Calm had been restored, and Monty was enjoying a nap after all the excitement with Soufflé. Megan secretly hoped the pig would charge back into the room. It was quite funny to watch. Plus, she thought Monty was coming round to having a pig as a friend.

'So, tell us about this truffle hunting!' said Dad, rubbing his hands.

'Ah, I think it is best to show you. You must join me tomorrow morning! Soufflé will show you how it is done.'

Monsieur Hubert's mood had lifted again, and he had a glint in his eye.

'That would be so cool!' gasped Nicole.

'Please, can we go?' asked Megan, hopefully.

'You have been so kind to us, Monsieur. We'd love to join you tomorrow, but on one condition,' Mum said.

Monsieur Hubert looked intrigued.

'You join us for a campfire dinner tomorrow evening.'

'Oh! Why of course! That would be lovely.'

The old man beamed at the thought of a day spent with company.

'I will even bring some of my homemade fromage!' he declared.

Megan thought back to the goopy, white, stinky stuff from the kitchen. She tried to shake her head subtly at Mum.

'That would be lovely, thank you,' smiled Mum, giving Megan a funny look.

'I will see you here at six o'clock tomorrow morning,' Monsieur Hubert said.

'6 am?!' exclaimed Nicole.

'We'll see you then,' said Dad, shaking Monsieur Hubert's hand as they got up to leave.

11

Truffle Hunting

Megan groaned at the shrill bleeping of Dad's alarm the next morning. She rubbed her eyes and shoved Nicole to wake her. Her little sister could sleep through anything!

'What is it?' Nicole croaked.

'It's time to get up. The truffle hunt, remember?'

'Oh yeah,' Nicole groaned.

Dad's head popped up from the van below.

'Wake up, girls!'

'What's for breakfast?' asked Megan.

'Mum's just sorting out some cereal bars and orange juice.'

'Ok,' the thought of something to eat convinced Megan to drag herself out of her sleeping bag. 'Come on, Nicole.'

Nicole sighed and followed Megan, hopping carefully down to the van beneath. Dad folded the downstairs bed away so that they could sit and eat breakfast at the table.

The air had a chill to it as they stepped out onto the dewy grass after breakfast. Megan was glad of the extra layers that Mum had insisted on. Their eyes slowly adjusted to the early morning darkness.

On hearing the family, Monty let out a gruff bark.

'Shh, Monty. It's just us,' Megan whispered, giggling as his whole doggy tent started to wriggle, his tail whacking excitedly off the sides.

Dad unzipped the tent, and Monty leapt out, absolutely thrilled by the prospect of an early morning adventure. He greeted them all enthusiastically, parading around with his favourite rope toy in his mouth. Dad fed him a quick breakfast, and then they set off towards Monsieur Hubert's house.

'It's creepy walking through the woods at night,' said Nicole in a hushed voice.

'It's ok…it's morning really. It'll be getting light soon!' said Megan, reassuring both her sister and herself.

After greeting the family, Monsieur Hubert led them along a winding, overgrown track through the woods that led from the back of his garden. Soufflé and Monty were both firmly on lead. Monty was enjoying the interesting new smells of the musky, dank forest. Soufflé trotted diligently at the front. She had the air of a pig who knew that she had an important job to do. Megan felt honoured to be carrying Monsieur Hubert's wicker basket, to put all the truffles in.

After what must have been half an hour of walking, they stepped out into a clearing. The overgrown weeds and brambles of the path gave way to a swathe of gnarly, old oak trees, only just visible in the half-light.

'La truffière,' said Monsieur Hubert proudly, sweeping his hand across the land ahead. *The truffle patch.*

Megan watched in fascination as Soufflé snuffled around in the earth, grunting softy as she went. Finally, she seemed to have found something and began rooting at the ground with her nose, burying her snout skilfully into the soil. Monsieur Hubert swooped in quickly, offering Soufflé a chunk of apple as a reward. She snaffled the apple greedily as Monsieur Hubert finished her work and dug carefully into the earth to find the truffle. He picked something up and brushed the soil from it.

'The treasure of Burgundy,' he said softy holding it up in the palm of his hand.

The truffle was about the size of a walnut and looked like nothing more than a lumpy brown rock. Monsieur Hubert handed the truffle to Megan.

'I can see why they are so hard to find,' said Mum in awe. 'Even if they grew on the surface of the soil, they would be completely camouflaged.'

'People *eat* those?' said Nicole screwing up her face.

'Yes! They are a delicacy. You can try some later,' Monsieur Hubert winked.

Monty tore himself away from the forest smells to see what everyone was looking at. He poked his snout towards the object in Megan's hand.

'Don't eat it, Monty,' she warned sternly.

Megan popped the truffle carefully into the basket. She smiled as Monty trotted along beside her. It was as if he was guarding the truffle.

'I bet they taste better than the lemonade,' Megan whispered to her sister, giggling as they followed Monsieur Hubert further into the truffle patch.

Before long, they had found three more truffles, about the same size as the first one.

'How much are these worth then?' quizzed Dad.

'Ah, these will be about 20 Euros each. But bigger ones, if they are in good condition, of course, can be over 100 Euros each!'

Megan's eyes widened. That was a lot of money.

'Wow, that's impressive,' said Dad.

'They say the demand is always much higher than the supply, so the price is high,' explained Monsieur Hubert.

'It's a lot of work to find them, though,' added Mum.

'Where do you sell them?' asked Dad.

'There is a restaurant in the village. Chef Marcus expects me to supply him with a kilogram of truffles each week.'

Suddenly, Monty stilled. He jerked his head up, and his body stiffened. His eyes were locked on something ahead in the forest.

'What's he seeing?' hissed Megan.

Suddenly, a flash of white shot through the trees.

'Is that a dog?' whispered Nicole.

The dog's curly white coat stood out against the inky hue of the forest. A man's voice called out after the dog, and they could hear footsteps coming their way.

'We must go!' announced Monsieur Hubert urgently.

He tugged Soufflé away and began hastily retracing their steps.

'Quickly, please!' he urged over his shoulder.

The alarmed family did as they were told and stumbled after Monsieur Hubert. Shouts and whistles rang out from behind them. Angry voices floated over the trees. Megan glanced anxiously at Nicole, who looked back at her wide-eyed. *What was going on?*

12

The Hunters

Out of breath, and with her heart still beating like a drum, Megan rested against Monsieur Hubert's garden wall.

'I am very sorry,' he puffed. 'Those men are not good men.'

'Who are they?' gasped Mum.

'The are fellow truffle hunters. Competition among hunters is fierce,' he said, wiping the sweat from his brow. 'Normally before light, it is safe.'

'Shall we go inside?' asked Nicole, nervously glancing over her shoulder.

'Yes. What if they find us?' asked Megan, still feeling rather jittery.

'They just want to scare us off the truffle patch. They will be too busy hunting now to care much about us,' said Monsieur Hubert wearily. 'But, yes. Let's go inside.'

'It's Soufflé I worry about,' Monsieur Hubert said, his hand trembling as Mum handed him a glass of water.

'These new hunters don't agree with my traditional methods. They think pigs damage the ground and spoil the growing truffles. But they do not understand how to train and work with a pig. They try to come here and take over with their dogs. Soufflé has been bitten twice before,' he sniffed angrily.

'Poor Soufflé,' Megan said as she patted the pig gently on the head.

Soufflé seemed calm after the busy morning. Monty lay beside her. He was zonked from all the excitement.

'That's awful,' Nicole said sadly.

'Yes, the dogs came after her in a pack...'

Monsieur Hubert didn't seem to want to explain any further, and Megan wasn't sure she wanted him to.

'They are very greedy men and do not respect the territories. I have hunted truffles here for many years, but I am the last of my kind,' he sighed.

'Is there anything you can do to stop them?' Dad asked.

'I don't think so. I try to go out before first light to get my truffles. I always stop at eight or nine truffles. That is more than enough to supply Chef Marcus and earn a living. There are plenty left if they are smart enough to find them. I worry that they will steal my trade with Chef Marcus.'

'What would happen then?' asked Nicole.

'It would be a struggle for me,' he said, his shoulders slumping. 'There are markets, but they are very far away, and I don't have transport. Without my earnings from the truffles, I would probably have to leave this house...' he trailed off sadly, gazing at the picture of his wife.

'Well, it sounds like you have a good deal with Chef Marcus,' said Mum, smiling kindly. 'I'm sure he wouldn't stop buying from you.'

'I hope not,' said Monsieur Hubert, standing up to see them out.

Dad gave Monsieur Hubert directions to their pitch.

'See you at dinner time,' Megan waved as they headed off down the path.

'I can't wait,' Monsieur Hubert called back.

It was finally light outside as the family wandered back through the campsite.

'Time for a bike ride!' Dad announced, clapping his hands together.

13

The Fromagerie

The family found the cycle path that led from the campsite to the village. Monty ran along happily beside Dad with his lead tied to the handlebars. After half an hour of pedalling, the pretty village streets came into view. They stopped outside the bakery and propped their bikes against the wall. Mum went inside to get a few things for dinner. She came back out with two long baguettes, three croissants and a huge slice of quiche for Dad.

'This croissant is *so* good,' said Megan, spraying flakes of pastry into the air.

Nicole nodded in agreement as they tucked into the delicious warm pastries. Monty sat salivating, longingly watching every mouthful with his ears pricked up hopefully.

Dad took a big bite of quiche and shook his head.

'Not a chance, Monty.'

Monty sighed, and his ears drooped.

'Oh, look! Is that the restaurant Monsieur Hubert was talking about?' Megan asked, pointing at a restaurant a little bit further down the street.

'The one that buys his truffles?' asked Nicole.

'Yes. Look, it says 'Chef Marcus's specials' on the blackboard.'

'So it does. It must be the same one. It is a very small village,' said Mum.

'Can we go over for a closer look?' asked Megan.

Mum nodded, and after they had popped their rubbish into the bin, they got back on their bikes. They pedalled slowly along the cycle lane. Dad was at the front with Monty trotting along the pavement beside him. Megan and Nicole were behind him, and Mum was at the back.

Just then, Monty's nose began to twitch. A bell tinkled as someone left the shop to the right of them. *Fromagerie,* read the sign above the door.

'Uh oh! Cheese shop!' shouted Nicole.

As the door was swept open by another customer, the cheesy whiff wafted its way towards them. The rest seemed to happen in slow motion.

Monty's head turned in the direction of the smell. Dad, noticing what was happening, grabbed on tight to the handlebars as Monty abruptly veered off in pursuit of the pong. The bike lurched sideways and clattered over the kerb. Somehow Dad managed to hang on, but he was accelerating towards the fromagerie, Monty pulling him along like a sled dog.

'Monty! NO!' shrieked Mum.

'M O O O O N N N N N T T T T T Y Y Y Y!!!!' bellowed Dad.

The bell rang out again as another customer exited the shop, carrying a neatly wrapped package of cheese. She looked up in horror as Monty and Dad hurtled towards her.

Monty flew through the air and expertly grabbed the package from her hands. He dropped it on the pavement in front of him and set about removing the wrapping from the delicious cheesy parcel.

Behind him, Dad had picked up so much speed that by the time he applied the brakes, it was too late. He crashed into the fromagerie window with a bang.

The whole street seemed to have come to a standstill to watch the commotion. The lady customer stood with her mouth hanging open. A slightly dazed Dad got off his bike and snatched the chewed up, half unwrapped parcel from Monty. Dad halfheartedly held the cheese up to the lady. She pursed her lips and muttered something in French.

Mum rushed over and apologised profusely in English and French at the same time. She went into the shop to replace the lady's cheese and smooth things over with the angry fromagerie owner. Thankfully, the shop window wasn't damaged.

'Are you ok, Dad?' asked Megan.

'I've been better,' he grumbled, rubbing his head.

Megan suspected it was mainly his pride that was hurt. It had been quite a scene.

They hastily left the fromagerie and Mum nipped into the grocery shop for a few more things for dinner.

'Right,' she said, emerging from the shop at last. 'Let's get back to the campsite. We'll need to get ready for Monsieur Hubert. We'll push the bikes,' she added, giving Monty a disappointed frown.

Nicole sighed as they set off back down the street.

'That was pretty embarrassing,' she said, looking at Megan.

'It was. I'm so glad no one knows us here!'

It took over an hour to push the bikes back to the campsite. Monty walked somberly with his tail between his legs.

14

Storm Clouds

Mum had laid out a selection of things for dinner. Dad had taken the evening off to recover from his earlier experience. There were baguettes, cheese, salad and an array of different olives and cured meats that Mum had picked up in the village.

Megan sat outside Monty's tent. She reached in and stroked his back. He'd hidden in there since their return from the village. He let out a sigh.

'It's ok Monty,' Megan said softly. But there was no coaxing him out of hiding.

'They're here!' said Nicole.

Monsieur Hubert and Soufflé walked through the campsite, much to the amusement of the other campers.

'Good evening!' he smiled. 'I've brought you some cheese, as promised.'

Mum took the cheese and thanked Monsieur Hubert.

'I'm not sure I fancy any cheese after the day I've had,' said Dad, as he offered Monsieur Hubert a seat beside

the campfire.

Monsieur Hubert looked at Dad quizzically. Then he roared with laughter as Dad recalled the fromagerie incident.

'Oh, that dog of yours is very amusing!' he said, dabbing his eyes with a tissue.

Megan was trusted to look after Soufflé. She walked around with the pig on a lead.

'It's not so different from walking a dog, is it?' she said to Nicole.

'I guess not,' Nicole shrugged. 'But remember how funny we thought it was when we first saw Soufflé at the cafe.'

Soufflé had taken an interest in Monty's tent. She nudged at the side and started to burrow her nose like she was trying to tunnel into the tent. Inside, Monty jumped to his feet, and the whole tent shook. Soufflé took a step back and grunted in surprise.

'Monty, I think Soufflé would like you to come out and say hello,' Nicole called in through the door.

Monty's head appeared in the doorway. Soufflé squealed and trotted towards Monty. Megan tried to pull her back, but she was strong. The lead was ripped from Megan's hand, and Soufflé disappeared into the tent.

'Oops!' Megan said. 'Monsieur Hubert, I've dropped Soufflé's lead!' Megan called anxiously.

'She's gone into Monty's tent!' Nicole added.

The tent started rumbling around. It wasn't big enough for a dog and a pig! Suddenly Monty flew out of the doorway, closely followed by Soufflé.

'Watch out!' called Megan as the pair charged towards the food-laden table.

Monsieur Hubert reached forward from his chair and grabbed Monty expertly with one arm. He called to Soufflé who trotted over obediently. Monty plonked down on his bottom beside Monsieur Hubert and enjoyed being petted. Soufflé snuffled about beside them, her lead now safely in Monsieur Hubert's hands.

'Now, that's better,' he smiled.

'We needed you in the village today!' Mum said, laughing.

'At least Monty's come out of his tent,' said Megan happily.

The rest of the evening went by in a flash. Monsieur Hubert had so many interesting stories from his lifetime of truffle hunting.

'So these hunters,' began Dad. 'Do you know who they are?'

'I think they are from the other side of the village. There is an older man - although not as old as me!' Monsieur Hubert laughed. 'I think he is in charge of the group. I have heard them call him 'Luca' but I have no more information than that.'

'Do they know where you live?' asked Mum. 'Are you safe?'

'Oh, I don't think they would hurt me!' he replied. 'They just want me to keep away from *le truffieré*.'

Storm clouds had gathered thickly in the sky. Big plops of rain began to fall.

'Oh, I should be getting home,' said Monsieur Hubert, looking up at the sky.

He wished them well and headed off home.

'Ok girls, get everything undercover and we'll get into the van!'

They rushed around tidying up as the rain got heavier and heavier. A rumble of thunder echoed around the campsite. Mum slid the van door open and they all dived in.

'Monty, come on!' called Mum. 'You're not staying out in this.'

Monty gladly hopped into the van.

'He can sleep under our bed,' Mum said.

'Ok,' sighed Dad. 'You are one lucky dog, Monty.'

Monty wagged his tail happily as he sat at Dad's feet.

'We love you Monty,' said Nicole, hugging him tightly.

'I think it's going to be a game of Top Trumps and an early night,' said Dad, taking the pack of cards out of the cupboard.

They huddled around the little fold-out table. Monty's soggy fur filled the van with a musty, wet dog smell, which Megan found strangely comforting, as the storm raged outside.

15

A White Van

Megan lay in her sleeping bag listening to the rain hammering off the roof of the van. She could hear Dad and Monty snoring in unison below. She pressed a button on her watch to see the time. 12.45 am. She sighed.

'Nicole, I need the toilet... Nicole!' she hissed, trying to wake her sister.

'Do you *really* need?' Nicole grumbled sleepily. 'Can you not hold it in until morning?'

'I *really* need. Please can you come with me? It's so dark.'

'But it's pouring with rain!'

'I know. Pleeeease.'

'Ok,' Nicole sighed, unzipping her sleeping bag.

They fumbled about to find their shoes and jackets and hopped down.

'Mum, we're just going to the toilet,' Megan whispered.

'Mmm hmm,' Mum murmured.

They slid the van door open and stepped outside.

'It's this way,' said Nicole from underneath her hood.

They squelched across the grass towards the toilet block.

Suddenly Megan realised that there was something else walking with them. It brushed against her side.

'Ah!' she yelped. 'Oh, it's Monty!' she breathed in relief. 'Monty, you scared me!'

'How did he get here?!' Nicole asked.

'He must have sneaked out when we opened the door. You gave me such a fright, mister,' Megan said, crouching down to hug him.

They located the toilet block and took turns to wait outside with Monty.

As Megan stood outside in the shelter of the building, she noticed headlights across at Monsieur Hubert's place. A white van was parked outside. *That's strange*, she thought.

Nicole emerged from the toilet block.

'Look,' Megan said, grabbing her sister. 'What's going on at Monsieur Hubert's?'

They could just make out two bulky figures bundling something into the back of the van. A familiar squeal rang out across the campsite.

'Is that Soufflé?' asked Nicole wide-eyed.

The van roared to life and sped away out of the campsite.

Megan gasped. 'What should we do?'

Monty let out a bark and took off in pursuit of the van.

'Oh no!' gasped Nicole.

They dashed after him through the sheets of rain. They ran out of the main entrance to the campsite onto a country road. Monty came to a stop as the van's rear lights disappeared around a bend.

'Come on, let's follow them!' shouted Nicole.

'Nicole, we can't. They're in a van, we'll never keep up,' Megan puffed. 'Plus, it's too dangerous. We can't be wandering about the road in the dark.'

'But they've got Soufflé!'

'I know,' said Megan, putting her head in her hands. 'We need to go back to the campsite.'

Nicole nodded. 'Ok, we'll get Mum and Dad!'

They sprinted back through the campsite. As Megan glanced over to Monsieur Hubert's house, she saw the outdoor light flick on. The old man came outside and started calling for Soufflé.

The girls stopped in their tracks.

'We have to tell him,' said Megan, casting a grim look at her sister.

16

Pig-Napped!

Monsieur Hubert's eyes swam with tears as Megan explained what they had witnessed.

'We're so sorry,' said Nicole quietly. 'We couldn't keep up.'

'And it was too dark and rainy to see the number plate,' Megan stammered, biting her lip.

She felt close to tears.

'The van was white,' Nicole offered helpfully. 'And it was longer than ours. And taller. I think.'

'Thank you, girls,' said Monsieur Hubert gratefully.

He rubbed his face and took a big shuddering breath.

'We must stop them,' he said, his face serious. 'Which direction did they go?'

'They turned left at the campsite entrance,' said Megan.

'But you don't have a car, how will you find them?' Nicole asked.

'I have a bicycle,' he announced boldly. 'Yes...I'll take my bicycle,' he said again, although there was a note of uncertainty in his voice.

Megan cast a concerned look at Nicole. There was no way Monsieur Hubert would manage to track the thieves down on a bicycle.

'Our van!' Nicole shouted. 'We can go in our van! Come on!'

Monsieur Hubert seemed reluctant to inconvenience the family, but it was the best option they had.

Mum jumped up when they entered the van.

'Where have you been?' she asked frantically, ushering them in from the rain. 'Dad's gone out looking for you...we thought you'd got yourselves lost!'

'Sorry Mum, we didn't get lost, but it's Soufflé! A van drove off with her! She's been pig-napped!' Megan garbled, the words all tumbling out at once.

'Get the keys, Mum! We need to find her!' Nicole demanded.

'Woah, slow down. I don't understand. Oh! Monsieur Hubert! What are you doing here...'

'Soufflé has been stolen, Mrs Bruce,' he said urgently, climbing into the van.

Mum sat down on the bed in disbelief. She looked at the drenched trio crammed into the tiny space. A bedraggled Monty stood at Monsieur Hubert's feet. Monty suddenly shook hard, spraying the van with mucky rainwater. Megan grimaced at the mess he'd created, but Mum didn't seem to notice. Instead, she snapped into action.

'Right...so you think we can track them down in the van?'

'Yes! Mum, please, we have to,' Nicole pleaded.

'But what about Dad?' asked Megan. 'He's still out looking for us.'

'We'll pick him up on route!' said Mum, clapping her hands and jumping into the driver's seat.

Monsieur Hubert and the girls jumbled the camping stuff and bedding out of the way before folding the bed frame back into seats.

'Let's go,' Mum said, as they clicked their seatbelts on.

They took the long route to the campsite entrance in the hope of spotting Dad on the way.

'What's that noise?' said Megan.

The van didn't sound the same. A clattering noise was coming from somewhere.

'I'm not sure,' Mum muttered, fiddling with buttons on the dashboard.

If the van broke down now, they'd never catch up with the thieves, Megan thought anxiously.

'Hang on,' Mum said, stopping the van abruptly and causing everyone to jolt forwards.

Monty slid along the wet floor and crumpled into the back of Mum's seat.

'Oh! Sorry Monty,' she said, as Monty let out a disgruntled groan.

Mum clambered up onto her seat.

'What is she doing?' asked Monsieur Hubert in alarm.

'I forgot to shut the roof!' Mum called down sheepishly.

There was a thunk as Mum brought the roof down.

Suddenly Monty let out a protective *woof!*

'AHHH!' Nicole yelled out.

'What is it?!' shouted Mum, losing her footing and landing heavily back in the driver's seat.

A face was peering in through the van window beside Nicole.

'It's Dad!' shouted Megan. 'It's just Dad!'

Nicole let out a nervous laugh.

'What on earth is going on?!' he asked, climbing into the front seat. 'Why was the roof up...why is the van on the move anyway...Oh! Monsieur Hubert?! Hello...'

Dad looked very confused.

'It's Soufflé, Dad. She's been stolen!' Megan explained.

'We're going to find her!' Nicole added. 'There was a white van. It drove off with her...we even heard her squeal!'

Monsieur Hubert winced. Megan nudged Nicole with her elbow and gave her a look.

'Oh, sorry,' said Nicole quietly, noticing Monsieur Hubert's discomfort.

'Have you called the police?' Dad asked.

'Not yet, we thought if we went quickly then we could track them down,' said Megan.

'Ok, let's go rescue this pig!' said Dad. 'We can call the police on the way.'

17

The Search

The van lurched around the twists and turns in the road. Their belongings slid and toppled on each bend. Mum was straining her eyes to see in the dark as the rain pummelled the windscreen. The wipers struggled to keep up.

'I can't see a thing,' muttered Dad. 'Did they definitely come this way?'

'Yes,' nodded Megan quietly.

'What's along this road, Monsieur Hubert?' Dad continued.

'It eventually reaches the next village, but there are many side roads before then...I...I...I'm really not sure which way to go,' he said sadly.

'Where would you go to hide a pig?' Nicole thought out loud.

Megan tried to put herself in the mindset of the thieves.

'Somewhere quiet probably... A farm, maybe? Or a warehouse? Somewhere out of the way,' Megan replied.

'Ah! There is a farm not far from here! Take the next left,' Monsieur Hubert said.

They bumped along an old track to a collection of farm buildings.

'I don't see a van,' said Mum.

Lights came on in the farmhouse, and a man appeared at the window. He watched them suspiciously.

'I shall go and talk to him,' said Monsieur Hubert.

'Be careful!' said Megan as he slid the door open.

The men exchanged a few words, sheltered under the porch of the farmhouse.

'I wonder what he's saying?' said Megan.

'Do you think he has Soufflé?' asked Nicole wide-eyed.

'I think that's unlikely, but he might have information,' said Dad.

Monsieur Hubert jumped back into the van. The family looked at him expectantly, but he shook his head.

'Never mind,' said Mum. 'We'll keep looking.'

After another half an hour of searching the side roads, they arrived at the next village.

Monsieur Hubert sighed sadly.

'I think that is enough for tonight. I can't think of anywhere else to look. She could be miles away by now,' he said.

Megan felt tears in her eyes and heard Nicole sniffing beside her.

'I'm sure the police will be on the lookout. They said they would be in touch tomorrow,' Dad said.

'I hope so,' Monsieur Hubert said glumly.

Monty let out a sad whine as they pulled back into the campsite.

'I know!' cried Nicole. 'We could try and get Monty to track her down tomorrow! He's amazing at following his nose!'

'That's a lovely idea,' smiled Mum kindly. 'But I think, even for Monty, that would be a stretch. I don't think he could track a scent over such a distance.'

Nicole pouted. 'I know he could do it,' she said, sniffing.

Megan reached over and squeezed Nicole's hand. She knew Mum was right, but she wanted to believe in Monty too.

'Monty could be of some assistance though,' said Monsieur Hubert thoughtfully. 'It would help me greatly if he could hunt some truffles for me tomorrow. I have to fulfil my order for Chef Marcus.'

'It's been a long night Monsieur Hubert. Are you sure you couldn't take the day off tomorrow? You must be exhausted,' said Mum. 'I'm sure Chef Marcus would understand.'

'I don't want to let him down... Besides, I need to keep busy,' he said.

'In that case, Monty would be delighted to help,' said Dad.

Monty sat up and panted proudly, then let out a huge yawn.

'Let's say 10 am this time so we can get a few hours sleep at least,' Monsieur Hubert said, patting Monty fondly on the head. 'Goodnight, everyone.'

Monsieur Hubert clambered out of the van.

'See you tomorrow, Monsieur Hubert,' called Megan, sliding the door shut behind him.

18

Truffle Hound

The following morning, once again the family followed Monsieur Hubert to the truffle patch. Monsieur Hubert worked with Monty, trying to train him to locate the truffles. After a few false alarms, Monty finally seemed to get the hang of it.

'He's got one over here!' shouted Megan, as Monty scrabbled at the earth.

But Megan wasn't quick enough, and Monty grabbed the truffle in his mouth before running over to the basket to plop it in with the others.

'I am very impressed, but Chef Marcus will not accept drool covered truffles,' Monsieur Hubert scolded.

'Monty, you just need to find them. We'll do the rest, mister,' said Megan, ruffling his ears as he gazed up at her.

Nicole removed the truffle from the basket. 'Eww, it's even got teeth marks in it,' she said.

Monsieur Hubert shook his head quietly. But Monty didn't seem discouraged as he bounded off into the truffle patch once more.

'It seems to be taking him quite a long time,' said Mum, looking at her watch.

'It's new to him. He is also very easily distracted!' Monsieur Hubert said as they watched Monty dart towards a butterfly.

'I'm amazed he's found any!' said Dad.

Before long, Monty seemed to have lost interest in finding truffles, and his nose was leading them all on a wild goose chase.

'I think that's enough for today. Monty is tired,' said Monsieur Hubert.

'But, you don't have enough truffles,' said Megan, looking at the small selection in the basket.

'Never mind,' he said sadly. 'I want to get back to see if there has been any news from the police.'

'Do you still believe it was the truffle hunters that took Soufflé?' Megan asked.

'Yes, I think so. I must track down this Luca,' he said thoughtfully

'Don't go putting yourself in danger,' Mum said fretfully. 'The police will be trying to track him down, I'm sure.'

'Yes, please come and tell us if there's any news,' added Dad.

They made their way back to the campsite and parted ways with Monsieur Hubert.

'Right girls, time for a quick swim before lunch,' said Dad.

'Yes!' said Nicole.

They raced back to the van to get changed before diving into the cold water.

Megan shrieked. 'It's freezing!'

Nicole laughed and splashed her sister.

'Monty did so well today, didn't he?' Nicole said.

Megan nodded through chattering teeth.

They looked over to where Monty was fast asleep in the shade. Mum sat with him, reading her book.

'It's a shame he didn't find enough truffles. Monsieur Hubert seemed disappointed,' said Megan.

Nicole looked thoughtfully at her sister.

'What is it?' Megan asked suspiciously.

'Maybe we could go back?' suggested Nicole.

'Go back where?'

'To the truffle patch...I'm sure now that Monty's had a good sleep, he'd manage to find a few more...'

Megan stared at her sister. 'Nicole, we can't! Mum and Dad will never let us.'

'We could just say we're going for a walk...'

'What about the truffle hunters? What if they catch us?!'

'I don't think they'll come back if they've stolen Soufflé. Surely they will be lying low for a while?'

Megan mulled over her sister's suggestion. It would be amazing to get more truffles for Monsieur Hubert. He was so upset about Soufflé.

'Ok,' said Megan. 'We'll do it. But we have to be really careful… and one of us has to be on lookout the whole time.'

Nicole grinned back at her. 'Yes!'

19

More Truffles

'Mum, can we take Monty for a walk?' Megan asked, pushing her empty lunch plate away.

'Of course! Meet us back at the van in an hour.'

'Ok, we will,' smiled Nicole.

'Thanks for lunch!' Megan said quickly, grabbing Monty's lead. 'Come on, boy!'

The girls rushed off in the direction of the truffle patch.

They sneaked through Monsieur Hubert's garden and made their way along the overgrown path.

'Right, Monty. Off you go!' said Megan hopefully.

Monty looked up at her and cocked his head.

'I don't think he understands,' said Nicole.

'Truffles, Monty. Go find the truffles,' Megan said encouragingly. 'Nicole! What are you doing?!'

Megan watched in amusement as her sister got down on all fours and started snuffling about on the ground. Monty watched intently.

'Is it working?' Nicole asked.

'Erm, I'm not sure...' said Megan, stifling a snigger.

Nicole made a loud pig noise and continued to crawl around.

Megan burst out laughing.

'Well, at least I'm doing something!' Nicole cried.

'Look! I actually think it might have worked!' Megan said in amazement.

Monty dragged her forward with his nose pressed to the ground.

Nicole stood up and brushed the dirt off her knees.

'Good!' she sighed happily. 'Right, I'll be lookout!' she called after her sister.

Before long, Monty had rooted out three more truffles, which the girls had stashed in their pockets.

'They're big ones!' said Megan happily. 'Monsieur Hubert will be so pleased!'

'Megan, sssh!'

'What is it?!'

Monty froze, his ears pricked up, and the fur on his back stood on end.

'It's the hunters!' hissed Nicole.

'Oh no! What do we do?' whispered Megan.

'I say we run for it,' Nicole said, looking intensely at her sister.

'Ok,' Megan took a deep breath and tugged on Monty's lead.

'Come on Monty!' she hissed.

But Monty's eyes were fixed on something ahead of him. Suddenly, a white dog burst through the trees, and Monty let out a loud bark.

'Monty! No! Come on!' Megan pleaded, tugging frantically at the lead.

It was too late. Three men came out of the trees in search of their dog. The oldest man called to the dog, which was now growling at Monty.

'Bonjour,' the man said, eyeing the girls and their Labrador suspiciously.

'We were just leaving,' stammered Megan, trying to cover her bulging pockets.

'You have truffles?' the man said, nodding to her pockets.

Megan froze.

'Give us back Soufflé!' Nicole yelled suddenly.

Megan shot a warning look at her sister.

'We'll give you all the truffles if you give her back!'

The man looked bemused. 'What is Soufflé?'

'Monsieur Hubert's pig!' Nicole shot back.

'Ah, the truffle hog. Why would we have the truffle hog? We have our dogs.'

'You stole her!' Nicole shouted. There were tears in her eyes now.

Megan stood rooted to the spot. She wanted to run, but Monty stood his ground. He was growling quietly at the truffle hound.

'She's pregnant,' said Megan quietly. 'You have to give her back. Please. You really can have all of our truffles.'

'We don't have the pig,' he said again. 'And I'm not going to take your truffles from you.'

'Luca, Henry's found some!' one of the other men called over.

'You girls shouldn't be out here on your own. Go home,' the man said sternly. 'I hope you find your pig,' he added as he walked away.

Megan crumpled with relief as the men retreated back into the forest. Monty gave a parting bark and then trotted after Megan and Nicole. They walked slowly back through the forest on shaky legs.

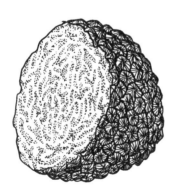

20

Bad Men

'You girls really shouldn't have been in the woods on your own!' Monsieur Hubert scolded.

They had stopped by to give him the truffles.

'Has there been any news on Soufflé?' Megan asked eagerly.

'No. I spoke to the police this morning...no news,' he said sadly. 'But, as I was saying, you should not have been hunting truffles without me! It was very foolish.'

'But we didn't want you to lose business with Chef Marcus,' said Megan.

'We wanted it to be a surprise,' said Nicole, sounding slightly miffed.

'I am just worried for your safety,' he smiled at Nicole. 'I didn't mean to upset you.'

'It's ok,' shrugged Nicole. 'Monty found some really big ones!'

'I can see that! I am very impressed, but I'm afraid Chef Marcus doesn't need truffles this week. I visited him this morning. He took the ones that I had with me but said he wouldn't need any more this week,' he shrugged.

'Oh,' said Nicole.

'That's odd,' said Megan.

'Yes, it was rather strange. He seemed quite surprised to see me... Anyway, I'm sure I can think of a new recipe for these treasures that you have brought me. They will not go to waste,' he winked.

'Did you tell Chef Marcus about Soufflé?' Megan asked.

Monsieur Hubert shook his head.

'No. I didn't want to lose my future business. Besides, I am hopeful that we can track down the hunters and get Soufflé back very soon,' he said determinedly.

Megan looked guiltily at Nicole.

'Erm...we spoke to the hunters in the forest,' Nicole said, grimacing.

Monsieur Hubert went pale.

'You put yourselves in so much danger!'

'Monsieur Hubert, the hunters didn't steal Soufflé,' Megan said gently.

'Nonsense! They are lying...I've told you, they are bad men!'

'I don't think they were lying,' said Megan.

'Yes, they actually seemed ok. The dog was a bit aggressive, but the men were fine,' added Nicole.

'We even offered them our truffles, but they wouldn't take them.'

'Those hunters are bad men. You should not have been talking to them.'

Monsieur Hubert sighed deeply and rubbed his face wearily.

'But if they don't have Soufflé...' he began.

'Then who does?' said Megan and Nicole together.

21

Chef Marcus

'Hi girls, how was your walk?' smiled Mum, as they arrived back at the van.

'I hope you kept out of trouble this time,' said Dad, raising an eyebrow at them.

Megan smiled guiltily. 'It was great.'

'We thought we'd go into the village for dinner tonight,' said Mum.

'Can we go to Chef Marcus's restaurant?' asked Nicole.

'Ooft, it's a bit pricey there, I think...' said Dad.

Mum frowned at him.

'But I guess as a holiday treat...' he smiled weakly.

'Yay! Thanks, Dad!' said Nicole.

'We'll be giving the fromagerie a wide berth though,' Dad said.

Mum laughed. 'Ok, you two, go and get changed for dinner.'

They were greeted at the restaurant by a smartly dressed waiter. He led them to a table outside.

'Dogs are not welcome indoors,' he said curtly, handing them some menus.

'*Merci*,' smiled Mum, taking her menu.

Her smile wasn't returned.

'Oh, look! Truffles!' said Dad. 'I bet they're the ones that you sniffed out, boy,' he said, patting Monty's head proudly.

The waiter looked confused. 'Your dog is a truffle hound?'

'Oh, erm, not as such...he was just helping Monsieur Hubert out this morning,' Dad explained.

The waiter looked down his long nose at Monty, who sat sniffing the air.

'I see,' he said flatly. 'One moment, please.'

The waiter hurried back into the restaurant.

'He's not the friendliest chap, is he?' said Dad frowning.

Monty was straining against his lead that was attached to the table leg. Something in the air had really taken his interest.

'Monty, lie down,' said Mum firmly.

Monty did as he was told, but he continued to sniff wildly at the air.

'He'll be smelling that fromagerie again!' said Dad, rolling his eyes.

The waiter re-emerged from the restaurant with a shorter man, dressed in a white chef's uniform. The waiter directed the chef to their table.

'*Bonsoir*,' he said, forcing a smile. 'You are friends of Monsieur Hubert?'

The little man raised his eyebrows, and his piercing blue eyes scanned over the family. His nose shrivelled up in a look of disapproval as he spotted Monty under the table. He forced another smile.

'Is this your doggy?' he said to Nicole, crouching down beside Monty.

'Yes, this is Monty,' she said, eyeing the man suspiciously.

Monty ducked away as the man tried to pat him.

'Chef Marcus, I presume?' Dad said, reaching out to shake the man's hand.

'Yes,' he replied, reluctantly accepting the handshake. 'I hear Monty has been supplying me with truffles. He is an... *unconventional* truffle hound,' he said.

'Oh, we were just helping Monsieur Hubert this morning,' said Mum. 'I wouldn't call him a truffle hound.'

'He does have an amazing sense of smell though,' said Dad.

Megan didn't like the way Chef Marcus was looking at Monty.

'Yeah, he's even tracked down bad guys before,' she added, giving Chef Marcus a hard stare.

'I see. Well, I do hope you enjoy your meal,' Chef Marcus said, flashing a fake grin before stepping back into the restaurant.

'He was a little strange,' said Mum.

Dad nodded. 'Maybe just busy in the kitchen. It was nice that he came out to greet us, though.'

Mum didn't look so sure.

The waiter reappeared and led a couple to the table next to them. Dad couldn't resist telling them all about Monty's truffles. Mum turned her seat to join the conversation.

'I get a bad feeling about this place,' Nicole whispered over to Megan.

Megan nodded darkly.

'Me too. There's something strange about Chef Marcus.'

'Monty didn't like him either,' Nicole added. 'He's really agitated.'

Monty was standing up again and straining against his lead.

'There's definitely something bothering him,' Megan agreed. 'You don't think that Chef Marcus might be...involved?'

'What do you mean? Involved with what?' said Nicole.

'With Soufflé's disappearance,' said Megan.

Nicole looked at her sister wide-eyed. She began to put the pieces together in her mind. It all seemed to make sense.

'Megan, I think you might be on to something...If Chef Marcus had Soufflé, then he wouldn't have to pay Monsieur Hubert for truffles. He could get them himself.'

Monty nudged Megan's leg. He stared up at her with his big amber eyes, his nose twitching furiously.

'Exactly. And Chef Marcus said he wouldn't be needing any truffles from Monsieur Hubert this week, but he must be getting them from somewhere...Monty only sniffed out a few, but look how many truffle dishes are on the menu!'

Megan glanced across to Mum and Dad. They were still deep in conversation with the other diners.

'Come on,' she hissed to Nicole. 'I think Monty is trying to tell us something.'

22

Sniffing out Soufflé

Megan carefully unravelled Monty's lead from the table leg.

'Ok, boy, what is it?' she whispered.

Monty's nose hit the ground, and he pulled Megan urgently down the street.

'Where are you three going?' Mum called after them.

'We'll be back in a minute, Mum!' said Nicole, smiling over her shoulder.

Mum's eyes narrowed as she watched them.

'I think Mum's on to us,' said Nicole.

Suddenly Monty yanked Megan sideways into a tiny cobbled lane.

'Oh! Monty, slow down,' pleaded Megan, barely keeping hold of the lead.

Monty continued pulling like a steam train.

'Monty!' Megan shrieked, as he dragged her up some steps.

'Just hang on Megan!' shouted Nicole, from behind her sister.

Suddenly a familiar squeal stopped them in their tracks. Monty's ears pricked up as the high pitched sound bounced off the walls.

'Was that Soufflé?' Nicole asked excitedly.

'It was definitely a pig,' said Megan.

A clatter from above startled the trio. Nicole grabbed Megan's arm and pulled her to the side. Megan dragged Monty with her. They looked up to see a lady at her window directly above them. The girls pressed themselves into a doorway to keep hidden. The lady leaned out of the window and shook a white sheet, before ducking back inside, clattering the shutters closed again.

'Phew!' Nicole exhaled.

Monty sneezed as the dust from the sheet floated its way to earth.

'That gave me a fright,' laughed Megan nervously. 'I thought it was Chef Marcus.'

'Me too,' breathed Nicole. 'Right, we have to keep going. Soufflé must be nearby.'

Megan nodded determinedly.

'Let's go, Monty,' she said. 'Let's find Soufflé.'

Monty looked at her and let out a quiet bark of agreement.

He led them further along the twisty lane. Megan was thankful that he had slowed down. Monty stopped to sniff briefly at a few doorways but eventually led them to an archway. He looked up at the girls.

'Do we go through here, Monty?' Megan asked, feeling a wave of anxiety.

Another squeal emerged from beyond the archway.

'Ok,' said Nicole. 'It's this way.'

They walked tentatively into the dark passageway.

'This is a bit creepy now,' whispered Nicole.

Megan looked anxiously at her sister as Monty continued to guide her along. The passageway soon widened into a dingy courtyard. A row of bins lined one side, and piles of crates and kegs lay abandoned. A steep flight of steps led up to a door.

'I think this is the back of the restaurant,' muttered Megan.

Nicole nodded.

'Monty, where's Soufflé?' asked Megan.

Monty sniffed furiously at the air. He followed his nose towards the bins.

Megan looked at Nicole. She hoped he hadn't led them all the way here just to sniff some stinky bins. But then the squeal rang out again. It echoed off the walls, making it impossible to tell where it was coming from. Monty darted towards the bins and frantically pushed his snout in a gap between them.

'What's he doing?' asked Nicole.

'I think we're going to have to move this bin,' said Megan.

Nicole sighed. 'Ok, here goes.'

The sisters grabbed one side of the bin each and heaved.

'It's starting to move,' puffed Megan.

'Eurgh. It smells so bad!' groaned Nicole.

The bin finally rolled forwards, and they managed to wheel it out of the way.

Megan gasped.

'Soufflé! What have they done to you?!'

23

Found

Behind the bins, in a cramped cage, was poor Soufflé. Her eyes were wide, and her skin was all blotchy. She began to squeal uncontrollably when she saw the girls and Monty.

'It sounds like she's crying,' said Nicole, holding back her own tears.

'We have to get her out of here!' said Megan. 'Sssh, Soufflé. It's ok. Please be quiet.'

'We need to be quick,' said Nicole. 'The noise is going to attract attention.'

Monty winced as the shrieking noise hurt his ears. He pushed his nose against the cage and licked Soufflé's snout through the bars. She seemed to calm down a little bit.

Soufflé trembled as the girls fiddled with the latch on the cage.

'It's all rusty. I can't get it to move,' said Megan anxiously.

'Let me try,' said Nicole.

Nicole worked at the latch, her hands shaking.

'Someone's coming! Nicole, quick!' said Megan.

They could hear footsteps behind the door at the top of the steps. Nicole frantically rattled and pulled at the latch.

'Got it!' she cried, just as the restaurant door burst open.

Soufflé stormed out of the cage, shrieking at the top of her lungs. Monty broke free from Megan's grasp. He lunged to the bottom of the steps and growled at the waiter who was standing at the top.

'What's going on?' came a voice from behind them.

'Mum!' cried Megan.

Soufflé careered towards the archway, sending Mum stumbling into the wall.

'Megan, keep up with Soufflé!' Nicole yelled. 'We can't lose her!'

Megan hastily helped Mum up and dashed after the pig.

'Be careful!' Mum shouted after her.

Soufflé's trotters clattered over the cobbles at a terrifying pace. Megan's lungs burned in her chest as she sprinted to keep up. They arrived back at the main street. Soufflé veered left and trundled up the pavement.

Up ahead, Dad and Chef Marcus stood open-mouthed outside the restaurant as Megan and Soufflé barrelled towards them. Chef Marcus made a lunge for Soufflé, but she skidded onto the road to avoid capture.

'Dad! Quick! Call the police!' Megan cried as she flew past. 'It was Chef Macrus! He stole Soufflé!'

Chef Marcus went to run after them, but Dad swiftly reached out and grabbed him by the arm.

'I don't think you're going anywhere, monsieur,' he said, reaching into his pocket for his phone.

Megan winced as Soufflé darted carelessly into the road. Several onlookers had stopped to gawk at the pig on the loose. A car blared its horn, causing Soufflé to squeal and leap onto the pavement on the other side of the road. By the time Megan had caught up with her, Soufflé had slowed to a brisk trot and was breathing heavily.

'It's ok, girl. You can slow down. I'll get you home,' she said.

Soufflé turned onto the cycle path and waddled slowly along beside Megan.

'Megan, wait for us!'

It was Nicole. She jogged up to Megan with Mum and Monty close behind her.

'Where's Dad?' Megan asked in alarm.

'He's at the restaurant. The police have just arrived,' explained Mum.

'Monty was amazing!' beamed Nicole. 'He stopped that nasty waiter in his tracks.'

Monty panted happily. He sidled up beside Soufflé and nudged her playfully. The pig wheezed quietly in response.

'I think poor Soufflé is worn out,' said Megan sadly.

'Yes, she doesn't look too good. It must have been quite an ordeal for her, being trapped in that grubby little cage,' Mum said, looking at Soufflé in concern.

'Will she be ok, Mum?' said Nicole quietly.

'I'm sure she will,' said Mum, squeezing Nicole's shoulder.

24

Reunited

Monsieur Hubert was overcome when they arrived with his beloved pig. He rushed out to the garden to meet them.

'I don't know how I can ever thank you,' he said, his eyes glistening.

He rubbed Soufflé behind the ear. She was still shaking after her ordeal.

'You're home Soufflé,' Megan smiled, crouching down to pet her.

Soufflé's little piggy eyes met with Megan's. She pushed her snout forwards and licked Megan's cheek.

'Oh! Erm, thanks, Soufflé,' Megan smiled, rubbing the pig drool off her face.

Monty jumped in to play with his piggy friend, but Soufflé closed her eyes and let out a wheezy grunt. Then she lay down on the grass and rolled onto her side. Monty lay down beside her and put his head on his paws, letting out a disappointed sigh.

'I think Soufflé has been quite badly treated, Monsieur Hubert,' Mum said gently. 'Maybe you should get the vet to check her over?'

'Yes. I will phone straight away,' Monsieur Hubert said, concern etched on his face.

'I hope she's ok,' said Nicole quietly.

'Maybe Monty could come and hunt for your truffles tomorrow?' said Megan. 'So that Soufflé can have some time off to recover?'

'I don't think I will have a market for them now that Chef Marcus has been arrested,' he said.

'Oh, of course,' said Megan, blushing.

'Are there any other local restaurants that you could sell your truffles to?' asked Mum.

Monsieur Hubert shook his head.

'But, I will worry about that another time. I just need to focus on Soufflé for now.'

Megan nodded quietly. She wished that there was *something* they could do to help.

Monsieur Hubert opened the door to go back inside. A cheesy waft rushed out to greet them. Monty jumped up, and his nose twitched frantically.

Monsieur Hubert laughed. 'Keep your dog away from my cheese!' he said.

'It smells different this time,' said Nicole, trying not to screw up her face.

'Ah. I'm trying a new recipe with the extra truffles you brought me. I'm making truffle cheese. A little treat for myself.'

'Oh, that sounds great,' said Megan, a lightbulb clicking on in her mind. 'Would you mind if we took some to try?' she asked.

Mum looked at her curiously.

'Of course!' said Monsieur Hubert in delight.

He disappeared inside to get some.

'I'm *not* eating that stinky cheese,' said Nicole in disgust.

'Yes, I'm rather surprised you want to try it, Megan!' said Mum.

'I don't. But I have a plan,' she said conspiratorially.

25

The Plan

They met Dad back at the van. He retold the story of his heroic capture of Chef Marcus to Mum.

'Wow, it sounds like Monty isn't the only hero of the day!' Mum said.

Monty grumbled from his bed.

'What's that smell anyway?' Dad asked. He looked automatically towards Monty, who sighed at him again.

'It's Megan,' said Nicole, pinching her nose.

Megan rolled her eyes at her little sister.

'It's not *me*. It's this,' she said, taking the cheese from her pocket.

'What have you got that for?' asked Dad. 'It's normally your sister who smuggles cheese in her pockets!' he winked.

'I have an idea,' Megan said, taking a big breath and explaining her plan to Mum and Dad.

'Wow. That's a great idea, Megan!' said Mum.

'I'm not going back there,' said Dad, shaking his head.

'It's ok, Nicole and I can do it,' smiled Megan.

Nicole grinned at her sister.

'As soon as the shop opens tomorrow,' Nicole said.

'I'm afraid you'll have to stay here though, Monty,' Megan said, crouching down to pat his head. 'We can't risk a drama like last time!'

His nose immediately shot towards the truffle cheese in her other hand.

'Oh no you don't!' she said, jumping out of the way just in time.

The next morning, Megan and Nicole cycled into the village and parked up outside the fromagerie.

'I hope they say yes!' said Nicole, crossing her fingers.

'I hope so too,' said Megan.

The bell outside the shop tinkled as they pushed the door open. A lady stood behind the counter. She was chatting in French to a customer, as she packaged up his cheese.

'Bonjour!' she smiled at them.

'Bonjour,' said Megan. 'We have some cheese we thought you might like to try,' she said hopefully.

'You can buy it as a new product for your shop,' explained Nicole.

'Ah, well, I only buy the very best,' said the lady, looking over the top of her glasses. 'What kind of cheese is it?'

'It's truffle cheese. A good friend of ours makes it...Monsieur Hubert,' said Megan.

'Oh, Monsieur Hubert! Yes, I know him well. He is a regular customer,' the lady smiled.

The girls explained the story to the lady and her customer. They stood gaping as Nicole described the previous evening with Chef Marcus. The lady shook her head and muttered something about Chef Marcus to the customer, who nodded sagely back. It didn't sound complimentary.

'Ok, let's taste this cheese,' said the lady, rubbing her hands.

The girls zoomed back to the campsite, peddling as fast as they could.

'So, how did it go?' asked Mum eagerly as they clattered their bikes down on the grass.

'The lady loved it!' exclaimed Megan.

'Yes, she said it was *magnifique!*' added Nicole, jumping up and down excitedly.

'That's brilliant!' said Mum.

'Monsieur Hubert will be delighted,' said Dad.

'Can we go and tell him now?' asked Megan.

'Yes, of course. Off you go!' said Mum.

'Monty! You can come this time!' called Megan.

Monty slunk out of his tent.

'He's been in the huff ever since you left,' laughed Dad.

'Oh Monty!' said Megan, ruffling his ears. 'There's no adventure without you, is there?'

26

Exciting News

Monty panted happily as they skipped round to Monsieur Hubert's house. They knew the path well now.

'I can't believe we're going home tomorrow,' said Megan.

'Me neither. I don't want to go home,' pouted Nicole.

When they arrived at Monsieur Hubert's house, there was a car parked outside. They knocked on the front door, but there was no answer.

'That's strange,' said Megan.

'I hope everything's ok,' said Nicole.

'Girls! Come quick!'

Monsieur Hubert appeared from behind the house. He gestured for them to follow him into the back garden.

'What's wrong?' called Megan, as Monty pulled her forwards.

Monsieur Hubert led them to a small shed behind the house. They could hear grunting coming from inside.

'Is Soufflé ok?' Megan asked in alarm.

'Oh yes, she is perfectly ok,' said Monsieur Hubert with a tear in his eye.

He pushed the door open, and they were greeted by the sight of a litter of tiny, pink piglets.

'Ooooh!' squealed Nicole. 'She's had her piglets!'

'They're so cute!' said Megan, watching the mini Soufflés snuffle around their mother.

A man stood holding one of the piglets.

'The vet is just checking them over, but they appear to be healthy,' Monsieur Hubert beamed.

'Yes. Twelve healthy piglets!' said the vet.

Megan counted the piglets. Eleven, plus the one that the vet was holding. Wow!

'Congratulations Soufflé!' Megan said softly, crouching down beside her.

Monty crept very gently through the straw towards them. He tentatively sniffed the piglet nearest Megan and jumped as it gave out a squeal before diving onto its mother. Monty settled down carefully next to his friend. His ears were pricked up, listening to the squeals and snuffles. Soufflé lay on her side, grunting happily to her piglets.

'She's amazing,' whispered Nicole.

'I can't believe the piglets can walk already!' said Megan in awe.

'Yes. Soufflé is going to be very busy trying to keep up with them,' chuckled Monsieur Hubert.

One of the piglets tottered its way towards Monty, its little, pink ears bobbing up and down. The piglet had a brown smudge on its snout. Monty looked at Megan for reassurance and stayed very still as the piglet curled itself up next to him and grunted quietly.

'Aww! Look!' whispered Megan. 'I think Monty's made a new friend.'

Monty looked at Megan with his head to one side. He wasn't sure what to make of this situation.

'I think I'll name that one Monty,' beamed Monsieur Hubert.

'Did you hear that, Monty? You've got a piglet named after you! Thank you Monsieur Hubert,' said Nicole.

'That's quite alright,' he smiled.

'We have something to tell you...' said Megan.

Monsieur Hubert looked at her curiously.

'We took some of your truffle cheese to the fromagerie in the village...and they would love to buy some from you every week,' grinned Megan.

'Oh my! That is excellent news. I don't know how to thank you,' he sniffed. 'That is a weight off my mind.'

'You could give us a piglet to say thank you!' teased Nicole.

Monsieur Hubert threw his head back and laughed.

'I don't think your parents would thank me! They have enough trouble with that brilliant cheese hunting dog,' he laughed, winking at Monty.

27

Goodbye

The following morning, Monsieur Hubert came to wave them off. He took Monty the piglet to say goodbye.

'I cannot thank you enough for all that you have done to help me,' he said. 'The deal with the fromagerie is the cherry on the top.'

'Can I hold Monty?' asked Nicole.

'Of course,' said Monsieur Hubert, gently passing the piglet down to Nicole.

Megan carefully tickled the brown patch on his snout.

'He's so sweet,' said Mum.

Nicole passed Monty up to Mum, who snuggled him in close.

Monty the dog watched them carefully.

'Don't go getting any ideas!' warned Dad, as Mum cooed over the piglet.

'One Monty is enough in our house, isn't it boy?' Dad said, patting Monty firmly on the side.

Reluctantly Mum handed piglet Monty back to Monsieur Hubert.

'Girls, I have something for you,' he said, reaching into his pocket.

He gave them a truffle each.

'Thank you,' they both smiled.

'The treasure of Burgundy,' he winked. 'You should get a good price for those in Scotland.'

He reached back into his pocket and took a big chunk of cheese out for Monty.

'I thought Monty might be the only one to appreciate my truffle cheese,' he smiled.

'Oh, I'm not sure that will be good for his tummy before the journey...' Mum stammered.

But it was too late. Monty chomped down the cheese gratefully.

'Bye, Monsieur Hubert,' Megan sniffed sadly.

'Please send us lots of pictures of Soufflé and the piglets!' Nicole called out of the window as the van started to roll forwards.

The old man nodded and waved, as the piglet wriggled in his arms.

Megan examined the wrinkles and folds of the truffle before her teary eyes made it too hard to focus.

'Well, that was an adventure!' said Dad.

'It certainly was,' sniffed Mum.

'The piglets were adorable. I'm so glad they were born before we left,' Nicole said dreamily.

Megan smiled in agreement.

'Can we get a piglet?' Nicole asked excitedly.

'No way!' scoffed Dad.

Nicole sighed.

'Maybe a puppy would be nice?' Mum said hesitantly.

Dad snapped his head round to look at Mum in shock.

'I think another dog in the family would be lovely,' she shrugged.

'Oh, yes! *Please* can we get a puppy! Monty would love a friend,' Megan gushed.

'We'll have a think,' muttered Dad.

Monty panted happily in the middle seat. He would *love* a new friend.

'Oh, Monty! Already?!' Nicole gasped.

Megan clamped her hand over her nose as Dad swiftly lowered all the windows.

'I told Monsieur Hubert not to give him that cheese!' Mum groaned.

'It's going to be a long drive!' Dad laughed.

THE END

Piggy Facts!

- Pigs have been used to hunt truffles since the 15th century.

- Truffle hogs can smell truffles that are 3 feet underground.

- Pigs are more successful truffle hunters than dogs due to their incredible sense of smell and obsessive love of truffles.

A truffle hog at work in France!

- Truffle hounds are being increasingly used due to the pigs being unable to resist eating the truffles!

- Italy banned truffle hogs in 1985 due to the damage they were doing to the earth.

- Pigs are highly intelligent and trainable animals - even more so than dogs!

- Despite common opinion pigs actually like to be clean - with the exception of taking the odd mud bath!

- Pigs are very social creatures. They can recognise their owners, respond to their names and express emotions.

Monty facts!

- Monty loves camping in real life, but he has never been out of Scotland.

- He has pulled Dad off his bike on more than one occasion!

- Monty's date of birth is the 9th of May 2016.

- Here is his mum with her litter of puppies — which one do you think Monty is?

WHICH LITTLE PIGGY ARE YOU?

Find the first letter of your first name and the
month you were born to find out!

The first letter of your first name is part one:

A - Bacon
B - Baguette
C - Rascal
D - Pork Chop
E - René
F - Oscar
G - Smokey
H - Gertrude
I - Wellington
J - Ogg
K - Hugo
L - Percy
M - Basil

N - Trotter
O - Martha
P - Molly
Q - Paulette
R - Squeak
S - Boris
T - Macaron
U - Sporkey
V - Sausage
W - Stu
X - Blissa
Y - Fleur
Z - Spidey

The month you were born is part two:

January - the Hairy Hog
February - the Porky Piglet
March - the Pygmy Piggy
April - the Pot Bellied Pig
May - the Muddy Piggy
June - the Hunter
July - the Mucky Piglet
August - the Truffle Hog
September - the Snuffler
October - the Hairy Piglet
November - the Portly Piglet
December - the Snorter

WHAT IS YOUR PIG NAME? MINE IS RASCAL THE MUDDY PIGGY!

Thank you so much for reading Monty: A Nose for Truffles! **Monty would love to know what you thought! Please leave me a review (or ask your grown up to help) on my Amazon page.**

For the latest Monty tales, competitions and updates don't forget to join my mailing list at <u>*www.claireowersauthor.com*</u> *and you'll also receive a free Monty activity sheet! You can keep in touch with me on social media too.*

We hope you can join us on Monty's next adventure…

Thank you for supporting an independent author.

Also available on Amazon!

About the author...

Claire lives in the North East of Scotland with her husband, two girls and, of course, Monty - the unwitting star of the show! Her sports coaching background helps her wrangle this  unruly mob. She loves working with kids, taking inspiration from their energy, creativity and brutal honesty. Recently, she completed an HND in Design and Innovation through the Open University and loves all things creative. Although born and bred in Aberdeenshire, she has strong family ties to Caithness and the Shetland islands and was lucky enough to spend a couple of years in France, attempting (and failing spectacularly) to speak French. All of these places have inspired settings in her books. She is currently working on the next book in the Monty series and trying to figure out Instagram.

References:

www.kids.nationalgeographic.com/animals/mammals/facts/pig

www.petpigworld.com

www.thepigsite.com

Printed in Great Britain
by Amazon

74386319R00108